INFILTRATION

CONNOR WHITELEY

Any questions about the book, rights licensing, or to contact the author, please email connorwhiteley@connorwhiteley.net

DEDICATION

Thank you to all my readers without you I couldn't do what I love.

CHAPTER 1

Superhuman Jackson Nixon grinned to himself as the small grey blade-like shuttle he was riding in banked gently to the right as it started its final approach to the planet below. He didn't actually like the shuttle that much because it might have been a little tight, as it had been designed for mere baseline humans instead of superhumans, the large metal chairs bolted to the grey steel walls were rather nice.

They were actually a lot better than other shuttles and it gave him the perfect chance to look at each of his "friends" as the five of them zoom down towards the planet below.

Jackson had always admired the fiery red armour of the Ignis Legion of Angels of Death and Hope. There might have been 9 original superhuman legions dedicated to the Emperor and protecting humanity, but now that 6 had turned traitor (including Jackson) there were only 3.

Of all the loyal legions, Jackson couldn't deny he

had always had a soft spot for the Ignis Legion. They were dedicated to order, fire and flame weaponry which Jackson believed was fairly cool. It actually made them interesting, unique and worth watching.

It even made them perfect targets for the first stage of the infiltration mission.

The rich aromas of burnt petrol, oil and even sage filled Jackson's helmet as the shuttle continued towards the planet below. He liked how the great taste of a good Sunday Roast formed on his tongue. He had never really known why the Empire Army had wanted to keep that most basic human tradition from Old Earth but he liked that it had been.

Jackson heard the hum and pop and bang of the shuttle as it started to slow. And even his immensely thick superhuman armour started to hum a little louder as it adapted to the mild increase in temperature. He didn't want to start sweating now and make a mistake.

This mission was far too important.

According to the Legion Lord of the Raven Crow Legion, the mission was rather simple. Jackson and a bunch of possible other superhumans were meant to infiltrate the Ignis Legion and get picked to be the loyal Angel attachment to a research world.

Jackson had no idea what the divine Lord of War and his Legion Lord wanted with this world, but he was under strict orders to simply sabotage the Empire and get all the information he could about the project.

It was hardly a bad mission and Jackson was

seriously excited about it. The Raven Crow legion were superhuman spies and Jackson never ever wanted to miss an opportunity to flex his spy muscles. He simply hoped that if any other Raven Crow Operatives were in the detachment then they didn't mess it up for them.

"We're landing in a few moments," a woman said.

Jackson nodded his thanks to the female Angel sitting next to him. She was apparently Captain Sadie and Jackson doubted she was another Operative given how shiny, well-adorned and perfectly in-tact her armour was.

It was standard procedure to go after Angels with battled armour because it was easier to explain the fighting after Jackson had stolen the armour. It was normally easier.

Jackson focused on the only other female superhuman in the detachment. She wasn't very short for a superhuman and her armour was twisted, battle-hardened and Jackson wasn't sure how well it would defend her in a fight.

Yet he doubted she was a Raven Crow Operative too because she never wore her helmet and there was such a fiery intensity to her eyes. It was rare to see that in a member of the Raven Crow.

They were masters of blending into the background, not drawing attention to themselves.

"Landing now," Sadie said.

Jackson nodded and all five of them stood up as

one single unit as the shuttle banged on the landing platform slightly.

Jackson liked how his visual filters automatically changed as soon as the shuttle's backdoors opened. Bright golden sunlight shone into the shuttle and Jackson was so glad to be on a sunny planet.

It was always so much better than the dull icy snow worlds that the Raven Crow Legion sadly had to call their home most of the time.

Jackson followed Sadie and the others out of the shuttle and he was really impressed as they went out onto the immense grey landing platform. It was just floating in the middle of the air with streams upon streams of white blade-like shuttles, cargo ships and the odd military cruiser flying around in long lines.

The military cruisers concerned him a lot more than he ever wanted to admit. It wasn't right for them to be on a research world unless whatever they were researching here was so deadly, dangerous or outrageous that it required military-grade protection.

Jackson grinned as his various stomachs filled with butterflies. He loved the idea of having to steal something dangerous and deadly so the Raven Crow legion could reaffirm itself as one of the most powerful legions in creation. He could teach the Empire a firm lesson and finally show the people of the Empire how weak and deluded the Great Human Empire truly was.

That was a brilliant idea.

"Angels," a very tall woman said coming over to

them wearing long white robes, a golden necklace and holding a kind of golden staff that Jackson knew could double as a weapon if needed.

"Research Master," Sadie said, "it is an honour to be requested for such a valuable and important task,"

"Now, now Angel. We both know you have no idea what we do on this planet and that is how it is meant to be. Your job is to simply stop the traitors from infiltrating this world,"

"Relax Research Master nothing will ever get through us. The Flame Protects," Sadie said.

Jackson forced himself not to laugh because it was clear Sadie had failed already. He really hoped that the Research Master wasn't looking too much at a possible threat though.

If Empire forces were actively looking for him then things were going to get a hell of a lot harder.

And that excited Jackson a lot more than he ever wanted to admit.

CHAPTER 2

Research Master Gianna Croft felt seriously sick as she watched the five superhuman Angels leave the landing platform in their silly little blade-like shuttle. She had never wanted them here in the first place but orders were orders if Regional Command was to be believed.

She hated the Empire at times, or she just really hated all their rules and regulations about her research.

Gianna watched the shuttle with the superhumans zoom away and she felt a little relieved that she didn't have to see them anymore. She wasn't against the Superhumans but if her pattern analysis had shown anything over the past few years it was that the Raven Crow Legion were great at infiltrating other superhuman legions.

She was sure there was at least one superhuman traitor in that small group. She just didn't know who and she seriously didn't know how to stop them.

Gianna shook her head and enjoyed the sweet mint, grapefruit and orange scents that filled the air as a light wind blew across the landing platform. There were so many calculations, sums and tests to run but they could wait an extra minute or two.

She wanted to savour this moment because she just knew, truly knew that everything was going to go to hell now that the Angels were here. She was going to have to keep them away from the labs and other vital systems.

Gianna took out a small blue disc and called up her assistant Roy Charmer. He answered immediately and his glasses were scorched so clearly there had been another failed test.

Damn it.

"I need options and tasks for the Angels. We have to keep them away from the labs at all costs. And how far until we reach Stage 2?" Gianna asked really wanting some good news.

"At least another few days," he said.

Gianna just shook her head. All she had ever wanted to do was to create a weapon that could kill all life on a planet and then immediately transform it into a lush jungle world. That was the problem with all planet-killing weapons in the Empire, it made a planet completely lifeless forever for at least more millions of years than she wanted to think about.

But with her weapon then there was hope that a planet could be useful to humanity again and nothing didn't have to die. There was a chance for life.

"We could create false attacks to keep the Angels busy," Roy said.

Gianna looked at the hologram. That might not have been a bad idea and it was the logical thing to do. The Angels were there to stop attacks and kill enemies of the Empire so if they created false attacks as far away from the labs as possible. Then everything would work out.

And how intelligent would superhumans really be?

Gianna had no idea but she had no intention of finding out. They did have some prisoners that were working for other labs and other organisations within the Empire. She supposed she could release them to cause trouble for the Angels.

"Roy," Gianna said activating a small setting on the disc that made it impossible for others to listen in, "I need you to secretly release the prisoners so the Angels will be busy,"

"Okay,"

"And I need you to get the other lab assistants to redouble their efforts. I am sure there is a traitor in these Angels and I am not allowing them to stop my research,"

"That's going to be hard," Roy said. "The research needs time and dedication. Adding the stress of-"

Gianna waved him silent. She didn't have time for this. "Prepare for a round of tests for my arrival. I am heading back now,"

"Wait," Roy said clearly looking at something behind her hologram. "The Angels are here,"

Gianna laughed and just hung up. She had never doubted the Angels were going to be hard to control, trouble or just a pain in the ass but now they were seriously proving her right.

All she wanted them to do was simply stay out of her labs and now they were there. They might learn what she was doing and they might even try to stop her despite all the regulations, laws and other things she had been "gifted".

Gianna went over to her own shuttle and headed back towards the labs. The Angels had to be stopped because this was her planet and she wasn't letting anyone question that.

And certainly not some dumb superhuman soldiers.

CHAPTER 3

The choking, overwhelming aromas of bleach, oranges and harsh cleaning chemicals filled the air as Jackson followed the others into the lab complex. The assistant Roy led them into the very beating heart of the research operation (the idiot) and Jackson just couldn't believe his luck.

It was lab was easily the size of four football pitches and Jackson wasn't sure if he had ever seen a bigger one. The walls and floor and ceiling were perfectly sterile and white. Jackson hated to imagine how overworked the enviro-systems were but that might work in his favour.

He got his helmet to focus on the immense hologram displays that covered the walls of the lab. It seemed the lab assistants and other researchers were working on some kind of energy equation. Jackson wasn't a scientist at all but the Legion Lord had given him some basic information so he could understand the basic science he might encounter.

He still didn't understand it at all.

There were rows upon rows of white plastic tables covered in different equipment, lasers and holographic supercomputers. Jackson had never seen so much equipment in a single place before, these people had to be doing some serious science.

And that meant if he pulled off this mission then he was going to achieve a serious victory for the Raven Crow. Something he wanted more than anything.

"I am sure the Research Master will be here any minute," Roy said.

"My concern is not the Research Master," Sadie said. "My concern is if me and my forces are going to be protecting something I want to know what it is,"

Jackson couldn't deny Sadie was a great Captain and definitely knew how to deal with baseline humans. He would have preferred to just kill them but that wasn't what spy work needed most of the time.

He started to access the planet's computer systems using his helmet to hack into them. There was a lot of encryption on the planet so much so Jackson doubted he would be able to crack it. It just seemed too intense for him to hack remotely.

A large red warning light appeared inside his helmet telling him he had been kicked out of the system.

Jackson wanted to swear or make a movement but he didn't dare. Such a small movement might have been the thing that gave him away and doomed the entire operation.

"What are you working on here?" Sadie asked.

"I am not allowed to tell you," Roy said gesturing to the endless amount of researchers and assistants in the lab. "There is more at stake here then you realise,"

"I am a Captain of the Ignis Legion. We know all about the horrors of the galaxy, you do not need to hide the truth from me,"

Jackson smiled because he really did love about that the Empire. They were all so arrogant, knowledgeable and if they knew everything there was about the galaxy, it was probably why they were so easy to infiltrate.

Jackson went forward. "What would it take for you to trust us?"

Roy laughed. "Trust superhumans, please. We would never do that,"

"We protect the Empire every single day," a male Angel said. "We serve only the Emperor and we protect the lot of you. Why would you not trust us?"

Jackson used the minor argument breaking out to focus on the large white plastic table closest to him. It was strange that there was a laser, a supercomputer and there was a bunch of notes left open on the table. It was something about life and what sort of bacteria or whatnot could survive a laser blast.

Jackson just shook his head. None of this was making sense and as much as he didn't want to admit it he was going to have to access the computer systems directly, it was just impossible to access them remotely. He hated that realisation because it only complicated matters.

"If the Raven Crow are here," Sadie said, "then we will find them but trust is a two-way street,"

Jackson really hated Sadie for saying something so stupid. Even if she was a Raven Crow Operative she had just said the most stupid thing imaginable. It was annoying as hell that she would plant the idea of operatives being on the planet further into Roy's head.

Or if she was loyal then that was a perfect way to make things more difficult for the Legion. Jackson really hated her, but sort of respected her too at the same time.

He knew he was going to have to kill all the Angels at some point but he was definitely going to give Sadie a quick death out of respect for her.

"I am ordering you to reveal your research," Sadie said.

"With me Captain," the Research Master said.

Jackson was just shocked when Sadie looked at him and gestured he, and he alone, should come with her to talk to the Research Master.

Jackson really didn't like this. He wasn't in control and that concerned him a lot more than he ever wanted to admit. Even to himself.

CHAPTER 4

Gianna flat out couldn't understand how stupid, pathetic and unforgivable these superhumans were. They actually believed they had the Emperor-given right to know what she was researching, that was such a silly notion that she hated more than life itself.

She led the two superhumans into a large oval conference room that she had never been in before. It was probably the only conference room with machine guns in the ceiling that could accommodate the superhuman's three-metre-tall height. It was hardly ideal but nothing about the situation was.

The conference room was surprisingly clean and Gianna really needed to make sure the engineer that watched over the Enviro-systems got a little pay rise. But she would have to make sure that did not detract funding from the research at all.

Gianna ran a hand over the icy cold wooden surface of the oval table. It was massive, clean and slightly rough in places from use long, long ago. The bright white lights in the ceiling above allowed her to see the dents in the superhumans' armour.

Even now she didn't feel safe in the presence of the two superhuman monsters. The Angels weren't normal and they should have been off defending humanity instead of bothering her and her project, the project that would save the Empire in the end from the likes of the traitors.

Gianna took a seat and shook her head for a moment as naturally the silly Angels didn't take a seat with her. She understood these weren't normal humans but it was basic decency or social norms to sit down when someone else in power did, surely?

Gianna gestured the two superhumans should sit and they did and thankfully the chairs didn't break. That was certainly one extra bill she didn't need, and then the enviro-systems made the sweet aroma of grapefruit, oranges and mint fill the air making the delightful taste of mint ice cream form on her tongue.

Gianna loved that engineer.

"You will never get away with this," Sadie said. "We need to know what you are researching so we can help protect it,"

Gianna just couldn't understand the Angel's logic. The Captain was a soldier and it was her job to follow orders, it shouldn't have been hard to follow the order to protect the planet. She didn't need to know what was happening on the planet in terms of research. She only needed to know who the enemy was.

Something that they all knew.

The Raven Crow Legion was the biggest threat here. Something Gianna had analysed a lot and she had come to understand the enemy a great deal, she only wished Sadie understood them better.

"Do you want to know why I am so careful with my research?" Gianna asked. "It is because my research, if it falls into the wrong hands, could kill the Empire,"

Gianna hated it how both that Jackson man and Sadie leant forward like that was something to hope for instead of a real fear. Then again these were superhumans, did they actually have fear?

"How?" Jackson asked. "This is a simple research planet,"

"That is how I have made it appear on all official records," Gianna said knowing hc would have looked up the planet before he arrived. "All the regulations and paperwork are correct for what I am really doing. It is the official records our enemies could hack into downplay the seriousness of the situation,"

Gianna got up and paced round the table for a moment. She didn't want to tell them but the Angels were proving to be a hell of a distraction to her research. Maybe if she simply told them what was happening they would leave her alone.

"Fine," Gianna said. "I am researching a weapon that has the power to destroy entire worlds *and* then regrow life on them. Instead of having Death Worlds that are nothing more than a lifeless husk, we can obliterate our enemies and still have a lush world. Probably more lush than before,"

Gianna hated it as the words came out of her mouth. She had never ever wanted to tell that because who knows if they were loyal and who knows what they would do with the information now.

They could send it to the traitors, sell it to aliens and just go rogue like other Angels had done in the past. Hell they might even try to carve out mini-Empires for themselves. Gianna just hated superhumans.

Sadie stood up. "Thank you for trusting us with this information. We will now review the security of the planet and plug any leaks,"

Gianna just wanted them gone so she could go back to researching whatever she wanted and she needed to call her boss, because things weren't going well here at all.

"Okay then," Gianna said. "Good luck and I want a full report later on,"

"The Emperor Protects," Sadie said as her and Jackson left.

"The Emperor Protects," Gianna said seriously knowing the noose was tightening around her neck. She had to get everything ready because her so carefully laid out plan was starting to fall apart.

She had to talk to her real boss. Now.

CHAPTER 5

Jackson was so damn pleased to finally know exactly what this research planet was so focused on. It was little wonder why the glorious Lord of War and his own Legion Lord had wanted him to come here because this was a brilliant opportunity for them all and a massive threat at the same time.

If the Empire managed to create this weapon then it could be used to annihilate them once and for all. He couldn't allow them. But if the Raven Crow had it then that could change the fate of the Legion forever.

"Here we are." Sadie said.

Jackson nodded his thanks to Sadie as she held a massive white plastic door open for him and the three others as they went into the Security Centre for the entire planet. It wasn't exactly the most modern security system he had ever been in.

Jackson wasn't a fan of the dirty white plastic walls with some awful art on them. Maybe the art was meant to be of seascapes, landscapes or maybe even a dog but it was all that abstract art rubbish from Old

Earth so Jackson had no idea.

Jackson supposed the view out of the huge floor-to-ceiling windows was somewhat beautiful for a human world. He could see for tens upon tens of kilometres as massive white shard-like buildings seemed to rise up out of the ground and create a skyline with a lot of depth and texture.

He almost wanted to know what all those buildings would look like if they were blown up or something. But he would lead that chaos to the Hydra Legion or that burning to the Galaxy Burners. He needed to focus on his own work for now.

"I have bought up all the records you need access to," a man said in a posh business suit.

Jackson focused on the very centre of the room where a large curved wooden desk sat with a tall man behind it and the largest holographic display he had ever seen in front of it. He might have had superhuman processing speeds but even his superhuman eyes couldn't take in all the information at once.

Something he had never ever experienced before.

"Thank you," Sadie said.

Jackson tried again to hack into the computer systems from here but it automatically threw him out of the system. That was just damn well annoying.

"We need to assess the security of the planet," Jackson said going over to the desk and Sadie.

"Of course my Lord," the man said. "I am Security Chief Terrance so let me help you,"

Jackson hated the name Terrance. It was such a weak, posh name that made Jackson really want to see how well he would do in a fight. He would probably scream like a child if Jackson so much as breathed on him.

It was so hard not to test that little theory.

"Bring up the entire planet and the routes onto the world," Sadie said.

Jackson was surprised she actually wanted to start there. The Raven Crow always focused on how deliveries and non-personnel got onto a planet because there was often less security for those items than people.

"We have two ways onto the planet," Terrance said. "There is the landing platform via shuttle like you came in or there is the spaceport. The spaceport complies with all standard and advanced Empire security measures,"

Jackson smiled inside his helmet because Terrance really was dumb. The Raven Crow was dedicated to overcoming such "security" measures. It wasn't hard to forge fingerprints, DNA samples and retinal scans. It was all child's play.

"Okay," Sadie said. "Let's presume the Raven Crow are more intelligent than I believe and they can actually get past those measures,"

Jackson looked at the other three superhumans in the squad and they were just standing there at attention. They were such simple soldiers that Jackson really didn't understand how the Ignis Legion ever got anything done.

Those three superhumans should have been thinking, asking questions and trying to contribute to this security check. It just went to show how dumb the Empire was.

"Run a check on the communications," Jackson said.

"Will do," Terrance said and Jackson liked how Sadie gave him a subtle nod of approval.

As the hologram changed to show a whole ton of transmissions coming into and out from the world, Jackson realised there was a single reference code that was private in nature. That alone wasn't strange because it wasn't weird to have corporate espionage happening on research worlds but every single week like clockwise the transmission went out from the world into space.

The receiver of the message never contacted the world itself and even worse the same code was being called now.

Jackson looked at Sadie and it looked like she was still analysing the data but he doubted she would see it. The Raven Crow specialised in data and pattern analysis, the Ignis certainly did not.

Yet Jackson couldn't start to understand what was happening with that reference code because it wasn't Raven Crow. The Legion never contacted anyone with something that could even be remotely traced and he had noticed a lot of corporate spies were already locked up already. So who the hell was this new player?

And Jackson really wanted to know if he or she was a threat to his plan. He partly hoped they would be because that meant he got to have a lot of fun hunting them down and ending them. Hopefully before they ended him.

CHAPTER 6

If those damned superhumans cost Gianna any more time then she was going to act and just find a way to get rid of them. They were definitely becoming a major problem now and she hated problems.

Gianna wasn't a fan of lying to Roy and her other close staff members about conducting a laser test in her private quarters, but it was the only way to make sure no one noticed or questioned why she was away from the lab complex.

She went into a small storage room right next to her apartment filled with more white metal shelves than she wanted to count. Gianna knelt down on the wonderfully cool floor and grabbed a small black holographic disk that was attached to the bottom of the very last shelf. She was relieved it was still there and it hadn't been discovered just yet.

She liked its solid cold weight in her hands and she activated it. A small hum of power filled the storage room until everything went silent and now

Gianna knew that she could be screaming out in pain and not even a stupid superhuman would be able to hear her.

Gianna dialled the only hologram the device was connected to and she simply waited for her real boss to pick up.

She actually had no idea who her boss really was except that she was called Sarah Oddballa. Gianna had been recruited by the strange, weird, mystic woman about two years ago but that was it.

Gianna didn't actually care if Sarah was loyal or traitor or anything. She was a good person who was paying for Gianna's entire family's cancer treatment so she just had to help Sarah no matter what how many lines and rules and regulations she crossed. Or shattered.

A moment later a tall woman in some kind of cloak appeared in red holographic form and Gianna felt a chill run down her spine.

"Good afternoon Gianna, what's the situation?" Sarah asked.

Gianna wasn't sure why her Boss was being so formal and nice but she didn't like it. She just got the sense that Sarah wasn't really like that in person.

"Five superhumans from the Ignis Legion arrived today. I am sure there is at least one Raven Crow Operative amongst them and that means we have a problem?"

"Do they realise you have been sending data off-world without permission?"

"Negative but it is only a matter of time. I covered my tracks well and if someone is Raven Crow then they will detect it. They are the experts in spy craft, not the Empire,"

Gianna hated how Sarah sighed in disappointment. She didn't want to fail the woman saving her family's life.

"How long until the weapon or research is complete?"

"A few days until the end of Stage 1 then maybe another two months for Stage 2 and another three for Stage 3," Gianna said hating how long this was going to take.

"Interesting," Sarah said. "I'll have to come to the world myself and deal with the situation,"

"Negative," Gianna said not realising how much authority she had put in her voice by mistake.

"Why?" Sarah asked.

"Because the Angels will be watching closely you realise and I do not want you to be captured,"

Sarah laughed. "Focus on the research. I will deal with the Angels and do not worry about little old me. I have been infiltrating Angels, Empire Army and even the Empire Palace for over a hundred thousand years without ever getting caught,"

Gianna was about to reply when the line when dead and to her utter surprise the little black device boiled away and turned to ash. She wasn't comfort with this at all and she was going to have to be careful for the next few days.

If Sarah Oddballa was coming then Gianna really didn't want to see her. It was only now she was realising how badly she did not want to meet Sarah in a dark alley at night, she didn't think she would be able to survive that.

She wasn't sure she would survive this research project.

Her communicator buzzed and Gianna put it on audio-only and was glad to see it was Roy calling her.

"We have a major breakthrough. There is a species of flora that was regrown rapidly even after a laser burst,"

Gianna laughed in excitement. That was amazing news and now they could move onto Stage 2 earlier than she ever thought possible. With the flora identified now she only needed to find a way to make sure the planet-killing weapon was able to deliver the flora for the regrowth at the same time.

An impossible task but something she was so, so excited about. She loved being a researcher for brilliant moments like this.

CHAPTER 7

Two weeks later Sarah Oddballa pulled her long grey cloak over her head and just grinned to herself as she slowly went through the endless crowds of little humans at the main spaceport. There were so many humans it was hard to make them out from each other but the smell of urine, sweat and poor people was just overwhelming.

Sarah didn't care that the security of the planet had been increased tenfold over the past two weeks, because she was always invisible to the Empire. Even now if anyone tried to focus on her the technology in her cloak would simply bend the light so it was impossible to see her.

She loved her access to the best technology in the Empire.

The immensely tall dirty white walls of the spaceport as the crowd tried to head off to the destination (Sarah really didn't care what their destination was), were impressive but Sarah was here for a single purpose.

Or was she?

Sarah actually had no idea why she had decided to come here. It was the reason why she loved herself, her mind and her career.

She was definitely here to kill the Angels but after that she had no idea. She could blow up the research buildings, blow up the world and kill everything or simply go and buy some ice cream in the canteen.

Sarah loved the idea of the sweet, creamy taste of rich vanilla ice cream on her tongue. She hadn't indulged in any real food for so, so long that she was so tempted. But she had a job to do first and she supposed she had a goal to achieve.

She just didn't understand what that goal was. She wasn't a fan of planning, she was only a fan of getting results.

And right now that meant hunting down Angels and killing them and hopefully adding their blood samples to her growing collection.

Little did everyone realise Sarah Oddballa was not your average enemy.

CHAPTER 8

The past two weeks had been an absolute nightmare for Jackson and he flat out hated Sadie and her tactical mind. She might have been Ignis Legion but she certainly had the mind of a Raven Crow operative, just not in the way that Jackson wanted her too.

He couldn't believe Sadie had spent the past two weeks hunting down every single threat to the research planet, killing them and making sure that the gap in security wasn't able to be used again. Jackson liked that about Sadie, she was clever, good and a great fighter.

She was just annoying as hell.

Jackson had tried time and time again over the past two weeks to get access to a computer system so he could get the research and be done with this mission. Sadie hadn't allowed it and Jackson didn't want to stress it too much because that was how he would draw attention to the fact he was Raven Crow.

That was why Jackson was going to make a new move tonight. Since the Raven Crow had taught him that if he wanted a different result he needed to take a different approach.

A basic Raven Crow tactic.

Jackson activated his night vision sensors on his helmet and started going down a very long narrow white corridor in the heart of the research complex. The walls weren't exactly much to look at because they were plain, perfectly sterile and the security cameras were thankfully deactivated.

The rich aroma of grapefruit, oranges and bleach filled the air so the enviro-systems had probably just finished another cleaning cycle. That was good because it meant the smell would be too strong for a baseline human for another hour or two.

He had time to be alone and he had time to get the mission done.

There were large steel doors with airtight locks on them as he went with little red holograms showing when they had been last opened.

Jackson wasn't concerned about the locks because he was a superhuman. One punch would probably let him escape but that would bring a lot of attention to him.

A door opened up ahead. Jackson froze and knew he couldn't be seen in the pitch darkness of the corridor unless it was another superhuman.

He noticed the lab assistant Roy was sneaking out of one of the labs. He was holding a large plastic box, maybe a holo-drive or something similar. Maybe he was the player wanting to steal information from the research planet.

Jackson silently sneaked up on him and grabbed him by the back of the neck. Not exactly the calmest of moves but Jackson fully intended to kill him anyway and blame him for the treachery. It would make his job a lot easier later on.

"What are you doing?" Jackson asked his superhuman voice booming.

"Damn it," Roy said. "I didn't want the Research Master finding out,"

Jackson pinned him against the wall. "Find out what,"

"Don't kill me. I am loyal to the Emperor I swear it. It is just this isn't good pay and another lab wanted the research,"

Jackson laughed. This was so stupid. The entire planet was meant to be secure as hell and yet there were more spies and corporate people infiltrating this place than the Raven Crow Legion. It was little wonder the Empire was in such a state when their security was so bad.

"Who do you work for?" Jackson asked applying a little pressure to his neck.

"Maxicus Corporate,"

Jackson shook his head. The Raven Crow had dealt a lot with that company over the years, they were "bad" people in the eyes of the Empire. But they had no problem selling information to the Lord of War and they definitely had no problem helping the Raven Crow legion infiltrate whatever organisation they wanted.

Jackson supposed he should have spared the man's life out of loyalty to his legion but it wasn't the Raven Crow way. And it would be a lot more useful if no one knew he was walking round after dark anyway.

It was even more useful to have a pansy to blame if needed.

Jackson snapped Roy's neck with just enough strength to get the job done but not so much that it was easy to tell that a superhuman had been behind it.

Then as much as Jackson didn't want to do it he left the holo-drive in Roy's hands because it would simply make it easier for Sadie to deduce that he was a criminal thief or a spy.

And that would certainly deflect the blame from him. But Jackson needed to access a computer terminal now more than ever before. Tonight was a bust but there was always tomorrow.

Jackson knew the noose was tightening around his neck and soon the body would be discovered.

And all hell might break loose.

CHAPTER 9

Gianna seriously hoped it wasn't true as she stormed up the long narrow white corridor towards the crime scene. There were tons of silly lab techs and researchers in their long white lab coats just standing round talking and blocking her path.

She waved a hand dismissively at them and she just wanted them gone. The overwhelming smell of bleach, oranges and grapefruit was annoying as hell now and even worse she could smell the subtle undertone of death that had started to be released into the air.

After pushing through more researchers than she wanted to admit she made her way to the front of the crowd and just looked down at the crime scene. All five superhuman Angels stood around the corpse of a man and Gianna could tell immediately that his neck was broken. Then she saw his face.

Roy was dead.

Gianna shook her head. She felt numb and

empty and cold. Roy was a good man, a great man and a very good friend. He couldn't be dead.

Gianna went over to the corpse and she felt how cold his corpse was and there was a holo-drive in his hands. He was a damn traitor to the Empire, the Emperor and the planet. She hated how the enemy was infiltrating her planet like no tomorrow and if someone like Roy could get into the heart of her operation then there was no telling who else could be behind this.

"Captain," Gianna said wanting some answers. "Report,"

"We're confirmed that Roy was a traitor and a corporate spy working for another lab. His fingerprints are the only ones on the holo-drive and there's no sign he was working with anyone," Sadie said.

Gianna looked at the other superhumans for a moment. They were all so focused as they stood at attention like the good little soldiers they were but there was one soldier that made Gianna feel like she was being watched.

Jackson was staring at her subtly. It was minor but Gianna had always been watched ever since she was a child by other boys so she knew the signs well.

If a superhuman was watching her when other people were not then Gianna had no doubt in her mind that Jackson was a Raven Crow operative. He was the killer and he was a problem.

"Captain we have a minor problem," Gianna said

focusing on Jackson. "I will say this once because I know I am correct but I believe Jackson is a Raven Crow operative and he killed Roy,"

Gianna liked how the superhuman took off his helmet and he didn't even react.

Sadie looked at Jackson and Gianna was surprised that she didn't seem concerned at all. Gianna doubted Sadie was another Raven Crow operative because that made no sense, she was such a loyal Angel of the Emperor so she just couldn't be a traitor.

"That would make sense," Sadie said. "That would explain why you were not on patrol last night in the area I sent you too,"

"This is a lie," Jackson said, "and this is not the way The Flame would want us to operate,"

Sadie laughed. "You speak of The Flame but I listen to you in your prays and hopes to the Flames. You lack the conviction, the hope and the drive that come to all Ignis legionnaires with such ease,"

Gianna waved her staff away and she saw Jackson still wasn't reacting. She had researched the Raven Crow a lot over the past few years but now she was getting to see one in the flesh. This was something else entirely.

She wished she had a weapon or something. Gianna had to protect herself, her research and maybe even her staff.

"Arrest him," Sadie said.

Gianna watched as the three Angels went to grab

Jackson but he punched them. The Angels slammed on the floor.

Jackson ran.

Gianna was about to order her security force after him when a massive red warning light screamed overhead. She called Terrance.

"What the hell is going on?" she asked.

"My Research Master we have a problem there is something in the research complex,"

"I get that," Gianna said. "There is a Raven Crow here,"

"Negative there is a woman. She's releasing the prisoners and the Hounds. And oh my Emperor!"

A large gunshot screamed over the communication network as Gianna's skin went icy cold as she realised Sarah Oddballa was actually here on the planet and she was killing.

She had just killed Terrance. Another good friend of hers who had a good mind, an interest in science and a rare true belief in the Empire. Something people lacked in her field.

But the Hounds were free.

Gianna hadn't thought about the Hounds for years and years because they were a joke project. She had designed them to be superhuman wolves and killing machines but they had never come to too much.

So she had frozen them and just waited until they needed to be released to defend the lab or something.

But Sarah had released them and Gianna knew

they would kill every single thing they came across.

Including her.

CHAPTER 10

Jackson flat out couldn't believe that damn Research Master had actually figured out who he was. He was normally so cool, so effective, so good at his job. This should have been impossible but it had happened now. And he really needed to regain control of the situation.

Jackson aimed his massive superhuman gun as he advanced down the long white corridor that sadly looked identical to all the others in the research complex. He wasn't sure why the Empire didn't want to change things up but he didn't have time for such concerns.

The red flashing lights overhead painted everything in strange red light that he supposed might have made a baseline human's head hurt. But Jackson had already changed the visual feeds on his helmet so he couldn't see the constantly flashing light around him.

He had to focus on getting to a computer

terminal right now. The mission might have failed because he was exposed but he could and would easily complete the mission.

Jackson stopped and aimed his gun as a small steel door opened and a little old lady walked out. She was wobbling along to herself as she went down the corridor without noticing him or the flashing lights.

He was half-tempted to kill her but he had to focus.

The woman screamed in agony. Jackson looked at her. She was being mauled alive. Ripped limb from limb.

Jackson just watched in utter horror as there was a massive wolf-like creature with thick black fur devouring the woman's flesh like it was nothing.

And he couldn't believe it as he watched the wolf get bigger and bigger with each mouthful of flesh.

The wolf looked at him.

Jackson fired.

The wolf charged.

Bullets screamed through the aim.

Jackson charged.

The heat inside his armour increased. A drop of sweat went down his face. The taste of iron formed on his tongue.

He leapt into the air.

He swung his fist.

Smashing into the wolf's jaw.

The wolf flicked its neck.

Chomping down on Jackson's fist.

Throwing him like a rag doll.

Jackson fired his gun.

The wolf screamed. Releasing him. Jackson flew to one side.

Jackson aimed at the wolf. He fired. Again. Again.

The wolf got smaller.

He charged.

Jackson jumped at the wolf.

He kicked. Punched. Fired.

Lumps of fur flew off the wolf.

Chucks of flesh flew off the creature.

The wolf hissed in pain.

The wolf charged as fast as it could.

Jackson charged a final time.

He gripped the wolf's jaw with his fists.

Ripping it in two.

As the loud snapping of bone echoed up and down the corridor Jackson just grinned to himself because he might have had no idea what the hell these creatures were, but there was certainly another player now.

Someone had released these creatures and given how they were killing every person they came across, Jackson didn't doubt Gianna hadn't unleashed them. She seemed way too self-fish and arrogant to possibly risk her own life.

Jackson continued down the corridor and hacked into the local communication network. Jackson really liked how the Raven Crow always made sure to monitor the local channels because the stupid Empire was always more likely to reveal important information when they believed it was impossible to overhear them.

"An Angel's dead," a woman said from the network.

Jackson hacked into the security cameras and noticed the woman wasn't lying as she spoke to her friend. One of the other Ignis Legionnaires had been murdered by a human a few minutes ago.

Jackson stopped dead in his tracks and he bought up a holographic map in his helmet. He overlapped the current locations of himself, the other Angels and Gianna over it. Then added in the location of the prisoners and whatever the Wolf creatures were.

It seemed there was a defensive line forming where the creatures were trying to stop them getting to. The main research labs were on the other side of the line and Jackson just knew that this other player was there.

And if whoever was behind this was using the wolves to stop anyone getting to the main labs then that meant they were after the same thing as him. They were after the research and they were after a computer terminal.

Just like him.

Jackson checked his gun and he marched off to find this new player and stop them once and for all.

They were interfering with his mission now and Jackson wasn't going to let than stand for a single moment. This player was going to die.

Even if it was the last thing Jackson ever did.

CHAPTER 11

Gianna couldn't believe this was bloody happening. Her life was a nightmare and this was costing her and her staff extremely precious research time. This wasn't good and Gianna couldn't help but wonder exactly how dangerous Sarah Oddballa actually was.

She went into her massive office with its bright white walls, white plastic desk and as she went over to it blue holograms appeared. Gianna scanned them briefly and noticed that one of the Angels were dead and Jackson was alive.

She didn't mind that for now, at least, Jackson might have been a Raven Crow operative but hopefully the stupid Hounds would kill him. Gianna looked at the holographic output of the latest experiments and she was failing again and again.

Gianna was tempted to go and rest on the various red, blue and purple sofas she had littered around the office but she had to stay alert. If a Hound managed to break into her office she had to be ready.

The overwhelming aroma of bleach, oranges and grapefruits filled the air and Gianna just went back to the holographic output. She had to solve this problem.

The problem didn't seem to have anything to do with the destruction of an entire planet because that had been done time and time again. The problem was all about getting the flora to regrow after the planet had been annihilated.

Someone knocked at the door.

Gianna looked around for a weapon but she didn't have any. She didn't have a holo-knife, a gun or a sword. She was defenceless.

"I know you're in there little Master," a man said.

The man's voice sent a shiver up on her spine. She knew the voice, she hated it. The voice belonged to Albie Scott, a former researcher she had arrested after he had faked data. She had managed to destroy his career thankfully.

"I'm going to kill you," Albie said.

Gianna tried to contact Sadie or a security officer but she couldn't. Communications all across the base were down all of a sudden.

A loud crackle echoed around the office and Gianna realised Albie was trying to break the control panel. Making the doors open.

The doors opened.

Gianna hid behind her desk as Albie wearing a black prison jumpsuit and holding a makeshift knife came in.

Gianna really wished she had a weapon. She had to find something or find a way to kill him before he killed her.

"You gave me a lot of thinking time you know in that cell. I wondered how to kill you a lot of times and you would be impressed with some of my methods,"

Gianna noticed he was coming straight towards her.

She jumped up and thankfully Albie stopped, grinned and pointed the knife at her.

"I'm going to enjoy gutting you and feeding your intestines to you before you bleed out,"

Albie charged.

Gianna ran.

Albie tackled her to the ground.

Gianna scratched his face.

Catching his eye.

He didn't care. He laughed.

Gianna hated his warmth against her body.

She punched him. She kicked him.

She couldn't do anything. She was a scientist not a fighter.

Albie rammed the blade through her left hand.

Gianna screamed in agony. The knife went so deep it was actually stuck in the floor.

Albie gripped her throat and Gianna just stared at him. He wasn't always such a monster he might have even been cute once.

Albie grinned and laughed and squeezed her throat and Gianna smashed her right fist against his elbow but it was useless.

A bullet screamed through the air.

Albie's head exploded.

Warm blood and brain matter painted Gianna's face and she went to scream but forced herself not to when Sadie appeared and ripped out the knife.

Gianna got up and held her left hand as Sadie got out a small first-aid kit. Sadie added small gel to the hole in her hand and Gianna was seriously impressed with how quickly it healed.

It still ached but Gianna was just grateful she could use her hand again.

"The gel contains superhuman DNA, hormones and other components mere mortals can only dream of having," Sadie said.

"Thank you," Gianna said. "What is the situation?"

Sadie laughed. "We have a Raven Crow on the loose and we have someone unleashing all this chaos on us. Do you have any idea who this could be?"

Gianna forced herself not to react because she was going to have to lie. She couldn't have Sadie turn on her and she couldn't have the superhuman think she was a traitor. Gianna was only a woman trying to help pay for her family's cancer treatment.

"No I have no idea," Gianna said.

"Fine," Sadie said. "Follow me and stay close."

Gianna nodded and she picked up Albie's knife

and just hoped beyond hope that when Sadie did finally twig she was responsible for a lot of this. That Gianna was quick enough with the knife to kill Sadie before she killed her.

Gianna didn't like her odds. Not one bit.

CHAPTER 12

Sarah Oddballa just shook her head as she sat on the massive desk of the security centre. Her friend Terrance's corpse was still in his chair and he was such awful company, Sarah had tried to strike up a conversation multiple times but he just wasn't talking the rude bastard.

She was currently watching all the wonderful action unfold around her and through the entire research complex. She had forgotten how much fun killing a superhuman was.

Sarah had managed to kill one and there were only four to go but the wolves and prisoners would easily deal with another one or two without her. She wanted to kill everyone on this planet because that would be a lot of fun.

But she supposed she only really needed to kill Jackson and Sadie. They were worthy prizes and their blood might not be that bad. Sarah still didn't understand why she wanted superhuman blood but she supposed if she ever had a dinner party her blood collection might be a great talking point.

She nodded to herself because the blood suited the rest of her collection very well and maybe she might add Terrance's corpse to her collection. Maybe he could make a new friend or two with the other victims.

Sarah looked at Terrance and his cold distant eyes stared back at her. She nodded because Terrance could be like that and it was paying off him that allowed her onto the planet in the first place (if her faulty memory was serving her correctly) so it was the least she could do for her best friend.

A small bleep echoed on the hologram as she watched Jackson was start starting to get close to the computer terminal. She couldn't believe he was being so stupid and easy to lure to a location. It wasn't hard to predict a Raven Crow operative would want to meet another player like them so she had already laid a trap for him.

Or had she? She actually wasn't sure if she had done that yet so she needed to go and check on that.

Sarah laughed to herself and kissed her bestie Terrance on the cheek as she left. And then she went hunting because Jackson needed to suffer, she wanted some blood and she wanted to see the fear in Jackson's eyes before she killed him.

That was going to be a hell of a lot of fun.

CHAPTER 13

As Jackson snapped the necks of two more prisoners, he was so damn glad he was finally making progress towards the main research labs and the damn computer terminal. He had already noticed a lot of different terminals he could have accessed but he really wanted to know who the hell was running another operation.

He wanted to meet this player.

Jackson aimed his massive superhuman gun as he went through a large holographic door that led into the main research labs.

Everything was completely silent as he went inside and even constantly red flashing lights were starting to die down a little. Or maybe he was just noticing them less despite the visual filter change in his helmet. He wasn't sure.

The rows upon rows of white plastic tables were perfectly arranged but the smell of rotting flesh, death and the vapourised blood that made the taste of iron form on his tongue told him everything he needed to know. Someone or something had already been through here killing the researchers.

He just hoped they wouldn't come back.

It wouldn't really matter if they did because even superhuman spies needed to kill from time to time and he had to complete the mission.

Jackson went up the rows upon rows of plastic tables. He noticed a few futile corpses on the floor but it was nothing he hadn't seen before. The humans were dead and at least that meant they could no longer help the Empire against his legion and the Lord of War.

He saw up ahead there was a large holographic computer terminal and Jackson went over to it. He bought up the research he required and connected it with his armour and started the download.

It was impressive as hell that a small pointless human mind could actually understand and create all of this stuff. It was fascinating to know how these humans wanted to destroy all life on a planet but also regrow it. Just amazing.

Jackson heard someone knock on another table and he turned around and saw a woman was sitting on the table at the very, very back of the room. It wasn't right considering he had only just checked the room as he came in.

He was a superhuman Angel it should have been impossible for her to sneak up on him and he couldn't see her. He couldn't focus on her. She was like a ghost.

Jackson had heard the highest-ranking members of the Raven Crow had access to these cloaks that bend the light to make them invisible, but he had no idea how a mere Empire person could get their hands on one.

"I would stop that if I was you," the woman said.

Jackson aimed his gun and prepared to fire even though he couldn't properly see her.

"Who are you?"

The woman laughed. "You humans are so obsessed with who I am, what I do and everything in-between. Some people call me loyal, others a traitor, even more call me a mad woman,"

Jackson really didn't like this woman. He wanted to know if she was a threat or not and she wasn't telling him. The damn woman.

"You might say I serve the traitors or I serve the Empire or I only serve myself,"

"The latter seems most likely,"

"Maybe but I like to think my loyalties, my plans and my actions are simply on a spectrum. I am everything and nothing on a particular day and today is actually going to prove that,"

"How?" Jackson asked.

Jackson hissed in agony as his entire armour crackled with electrical energy as the download was complete. His armour malfunctioned and sent deadly electrical energy into his flesh and his superhuman hearts struggled to keep pumping.

His muscles stopped working and he collapsed to the ground, with his armour not working Jackson hated how each movement felt like he was moving an entire planet with just his arms.

He couldn't do it.

The woman stood over him. "I tried to warn you. I didn't want you to download my virus that looked like research but you didn't listen. Why don't you listen?"

Jackson wanted to kill the damn woman but he couldn't move his body because of the sheer weight of his armour.

"It doesn't matter," the woman said. "The point is that you are here now and I get to play with you and your flesh. I wonder how good your blood is I would love a blood sample from you,"

"Why?"

The woman laughed. "I don't have a fucking clue,"

Jackson's stomachs twisted into a painful knot as the woman started unnaturally dragging him along like he was weightless. Jackson hated this woman, he feared this woman and he couldn't believe it. But he really wanted Sadie to come and save him.

And to hell with the consequences.

CHAPTER 14

Gianna flat out hated how the situation was falling down around her. All she had wanted to do some research but now everything was falling apart.

Gianna stood next to Sadie as they stared at the two corpses of Sadie's friends at an awful fork in four corridors. She was surprised at how massive the corpses of superhumans were and how badly cracked their fiery red armour was. This was awful and it was scary as hell to actually realise some of humanity's greatest warriors could die.

Maybe like the rest of humanity, Gianna had believed deep, deep down that the Angels were the unkillable defenders of humanity. Something that was very much a myth right now and maybe it had always been.

Gianna was glad when the red flashing lights stopped and she knew some of her surviving staff members were trying to reboot the computer systems. Anything to get the damn communication network back online.

"We need to move out," Sadie said.

"But your friends?"

"They are dead. They died in service to the Emperor there is nothing more that can be done for them now. The fate of my legion's honour now depends on me,"

Gianna shook her head. She had always known the coldness of superhumans was fact and she knew she could be cold at times but these were meant to be her friends. And Sadie didn't care.

Then she realised.

"How long have you been Raven Crow?" Gianna asked subtly trying to decide which way she was going to run.

Sadie laughed. "What makes you think I am Raven Crow? There are nine so-called traitor legions and three so-called loyal ones,"

"A free agent then?" Gianna asked really hating the situation she was in. She wished she was a fighter for a change and not a scientist.

"Maybe," Sadie said pointing her gun at Gianna. "You realise there are a lot of organisations that would pay for you, your mind and your research. Some Empire, some traitor, some alien,"

Gianna shook her head and backed away. "You had all of us fooled,"

"Incorrect, I doubt I fooled Jackson but he probably believes I'm Raven Crow like him. It doesn't matter because I will kill you, get the research and leave this planet without anyone realising what has truly happened,"

Gianna backed away a little more. "But then you will never be able to return to your Legion again? I thought-"

Sadie waved her silent but Gianna hated being silenced by someone as pointless and dumb as a superhuman.

"I thought the Angels loved the Emperor and their legion. The legion is their family,"

"We can choose and kill your families as easily as we form them. My legion was good to me but there is an entire galaxy out there to explore. The Empire is a rotting corpse that will be dead soon enough,"

Gianna pointed her knife at Sadie. It looked pathetic compared to the bulk of the superhuman.

Sadie laughed and simply walked away.

"Sarah Oddballa is here," Gianna said not knowing if that meant something to the superhuman.

Sadie stopped and sighed. "I was wondering when the step-mother of Angels would turn up once more. She will be killed just like you,"

Gianna just watched as Sadie walked away shaking her head. She had no idea what Sadie meant about Sarah being the Step-Mother of Angels. The Angels of Death and Hope had been created by Doctor Catherine Taylor, she was the Mother of Angels. So why did they need a stepmother?

A Hound roared behind her.

Gianna spun around.

The Hound launched itself at her.

She slashed her knife.

The Hound screamed.

Blood splattered up walls.

The Hound collapsed on the ground and hissed in pain a little.

Gianna went over and thrusted her knife into the spinal cord, killing the Hound instantly.

"I'm going to kill you," a woman said her voice echoing all around the four corners.

Gianna just shook her head because enough was enough. She had Jackson trying to steal the information for the traitors, she had a mad Sarah Oddballa trying to steal the information for Emperor knows what purpose and now she had Sadie wanting to still the information for her own purposes.

She needed this all to end and that meant she was going to have to use the research from Stage 1. She needed to activate the prototype of the planet-killing weapon that she had made and designed herself.

She couldn't allow anyone to escape this planet alive.

Herself included.

CHAPTER 15

Jackson hated how the stupid Sarah woman had decided to push together eight different white plastic tables to form a slab for her to perform whatever foul surgery she wanted to do.

Jackson wanted to fight, kill, just do something to save himself but he didn't have the strength now that his armour didn't have any power. He had always known it was the mixture of his armour and skill that made him a great killer and spy but now he was useless.

"Please don't scream," Sarah said.

The icy coldness of the plastic table made him shiver as Sarah got out a range of holo-knives and started slicing off his armour. Jackson hissed in pain as he felt the extreme heat of the holo-knife slice his skin as she didn't care if he was hurt or not. The awful smell of bleach, oranges and grapefruit was really starting to annoy him now and Jackson just wanted to smell the dead body of Sarah.

At least it would change things up a little.

"Here you go," Sarah said as she removed Jackson's armour around his hands. "Such pretty fingers,"

Jackson started to move around and he was surprised at how cold the air was. The enviro-systems should have stopped that and helped to maintain the temperature. Something was seriously wrong here.

"What's your plans for this world?" Jackson asked.

Sarah shrugged. "Considering I lie to everyone even myself there is no point my darling in answering your query,"

Jackson moved his fingers more and more until Sarah sliced off his forefingers.

Sarah held them up like they were expert specimens of something she wanted to study. "Will you look at that? Two fingers belonging to the Raven Crow. That is fascinating,"

"At least you have your blood samples," Jackson said hissing through the pain.

"Blood samples?" Sarah asked. "I don't care about blood samples. Wait? Do I? Did I say that?"

Jackson had no idea what the hell this woman was but she was crazy or at least extremely unreliable.

Jackson threw his arm towards her but his arm just stopped about a centimetre from her face. Sarah laughed as the sound of a holo-chain buzzing next to him made him roll his eyes.

He hadn't realised he had been so busy focusing

on killing her that she had attached a chain to him. The clever bastard.

"What do you want with the research?" Jackson asked watching Sarah start to remove the armour around his arms.

"I don't want anything with it,"

"Then why come here? Why come to this planet and want to burn and fight and do whatever you're doing."

"Because I get bored easily and I'm a very obsessive and compulsive person. If I feel like I do something then I do it and be damned with the consequences. I don't know why I want the research but I just do,"

"I thought you said you didn't want the research,"

Sarah laughed and shrugged. "See I lie all the time even to myself,"

"Is that a lie?" Jackson asked smiling as she removed the armour around his arms.

"I have no idea darling,"

Jackson noticed the holo-chain was attached to his shoulder armour, something Sarah had also just removed.

He swung his arm towards her.

She shot back.

Jackson sat up.

He was strong enough to move.

He stood up. Hating the pain in his joints as he moved.

Sarah whipped out a gun.

She fired.

Jackson dived to one side.

Sarah ran towards the door.

Jackson leapt up.

He chased after her.

He leapt over tables.

Over bodies.

Over everything.

Sadie appeared in the doorway.

Sarah shot her.

Bullets screamed through the air.

Smashing into Sadie's armour.

Jackson leapt through the air.

Sarah leapt over Sadie.

Sarah ran away.

Sadie collapsed to the ground.

Thick dark red superhuman blood poured out of her stomach. And as much as Jackson wanted to chase after Sarah he knew she was already gone.

Sadie reached out a hand for Jackson and he was surprised when Sadie took off her helmet and smiled at him. Jackson liked the warmth, authority and devotion to the Emperor in her eyes.

But ultimately he knew she wasn't Ignis Legion, she wasn't Raven Crow, she was a Free Agent. She had turned her back on the legion ages ago, that much was clear, but she was still stupidly loyal to the Emperor.

Jackson knelt down next to her. "You are a fool

for siding with him,"

Sadie laughed. "You're going to give me a hard time now traitor? You have to find Gianna and kill her, forget Sarah. I studied Gianna a lot before I came here,"

"Why?"

"Because," Sadie said, "the Empire might be dying because they refuse to learn from the enemy. But I understand Raven Crow tactics, always know your enemy better than yourself,"

Jackson was almost a little proud of her.

"Gianna would be hopeless about now and she would want to deny all of us the research,"

"Then let her kill the planet. The research is useless anyway. It will not change anything,"

Sadie laughed. "At the end of this, explore the computer systems because there are copies of the original plans that the Emperor created when he was making the Angels,"

Jackson stood up and shook his head. He would never deny that his legion and the other so-called traitor legions had lost the ability to create new Angels long, long ago but if what Sadie said was true. Then there was a chance the Legions could regrow again and become an even greater threat to the Empire.

"Thank you," Jackson said taking Sadie's gun. "You aren't so bad for a loyalist,"

"Just kill Gianna and kill Sarah if you have a chance,"

"What would your legion say? The Flame Protects?"

"And the Emperor Protects," Sadie said.

"Fuck off I'm not saying that,"

Jackson just smiled as he went down and just listened to Sadie's laughter as she died and he went off to hunt down Gianna. This game ended now and Gianna had to die.

There was simply no other choice.

But little did everyone realise that no plan was ever easy when Sarah Oddballa was about.

CHAPTER 16

Gianna hated that she was going to do this but damn Sarah Oddballa had simply left her no choice. She had tried to figure out another way but none of her other options were very effective. She had to kill everyone and make sure Sarah Oddballa died tonight.

She hissed in pain as she grabbed the icy cold metal handle of the white column that contained the computer system controlling the laser weapon section of the research project. The temperature was so cold for some reason and Gianna couldn't understand why.

The drops of cold sweat that had been rolling down her back had formed into ice and as her hands turned the handle they started to shiver. The white walls of the small chamber were covered in ice shards and Gianna really wanted to hurry up.

After a few moments the handle finished turning by itself and the metal column dissolved into the floor to reveal the small holographic computer. The computer that would allow her to make everything right with the world and kill Sarah.

Something she should have done ages ago.

The choking aroma of bleach, grapefruits and oranges filled the air so intensely that Gianna coughed again and again. Her eyes streamed tears as the vapour clawed at her throat.

She turned around but Sarah was standing right there.

Sarah was grinning at her and she seemed completely unaffected by everything. Gianna didn't doubt she had a rebreather on or something but that damn cloak made it impossible to see her face clearly.

All except for her awful smile.

Gianna went down onto her knees and gasped for air. Her vision blurred as the tears became too much.

"You know that's what I like about superhumans," Sarah said coming over to the holographic computer. "I like that they can survive anything unlike you weaker humans,"

"What are you?"

"Me? Oh, I don't know I might be a baseline human, I might be a superhuman. I might be an alien like the Emperor. Ha. That would be a lot of fun to realise that,"

Gianna went to grab Sarah's cloak but her hand simply went straight through where she thought a piece of her cloak was. She just couldn't see Sarah clearly enough.

"Thank you for the gift," Sarah said.

Gianna noticed how the awful aromas went away and Gianna wiped her eyes and focused on the foul look at Sarah. She had deactivated her technology that deflected the light. Gianna hated her.

Sarah's smooth beautiful features looked too perfect, too smooth, too elegant to belong to such a foul woman. And even worse she was actually holding the holographic computer.

The technology that would allow her to kill the entire planet or use the laser technology however she saw fit. Something Gianna was fairly sure wasn't a concept in Sarah's mind.

"Goodbye," Sarah said.

Gianna flinched. "What are you going to do with it?"

Sarah shrugged. "I'm a madwoman. I can only use this thing outside on the roof so I have until I reach the roof to decide,"

"Lord Commander," a man said over Sarah's communication device, "we have received your summons. What's the situation? Have the aliens broken through the line?"

Gianna frowned as she realised Sarah had somehow managed to convince an entire battle force of the Empire Army to come to the planet. That had to easily be ten thousand innocent lives that Sarah was probably going to kill for the fun of it.

"That's why you needed the communication system down," Gianna said standing up. "You needed to broadcast your lies to get them here,"

Sarah shrugged. "Maybe I did. Maybe I didn't. Maybe I just cannot remember or maybe I just lie a lot,"

Sarah whipped out a pistol.

Gianna whipped out her holo-knife. She noticed a shadow moved in the doorway.

"You really want to bring a knife to a gun fight kid?" Sarah asked.

"I don't need to kill you. That's what a superhuman's for,"

Sarah shook her head as Jackson stormed in. His gun blazing.

Sarah clicked her fingers and blue tendrils of smoke twirled, whirled and swirled around her and she simply teleported away.

"Damn it," Gianna said as Jackson stopped in front of her.

"What is her plan?"

Gianna laughed. "I don't even think she fucking has one. She's a madwoman but there is an entire fleet of Empire Army warships incoming,"

Jackson nodded. "That would make sense. If she destroyed the planet and the warships were near enough then she could easily take them out too,"

"We have to stop her together," Gianna said hating how she was even suggesting such an outrageous action.

"Well a so-called traitor and a Research Master," Jackson said hating the suggestion, "working together.

No one will ever see that coming,"

Gianna extended her hand and as much as she hated this idea. It was the only way to stop Sarah, save the innocent lives in the Battle Force and hopefully stop Jackson in the process.

"Truce," Gianna said.

"Truce," Jackson said. "For the Lord of War and the Legion That Goes Bump In The Night,"

"For the Emperor," Gianna said knowing she had just made a deal with the devil.

But she was too smart to think Jackson was a good devil, demon or whatever. She knew he would betray her first given the opportunity so she was going to have to kill him.

No matter what the consequences were and no matter how badly it increased the chance of her own death. The Empire was far too important, wasn't it?

CHAPTER 17

As Jackson and Gianna raced up the long metal staircase towards the circular landing platform on the roof of the research complex, he flat out couldn't believe Gianna was so stupid to trust him.

As soon as this was over he was going to access the computer systems regardless of what she said and he was going to download all the research about creating new Angels. That was critical for the so-called Traitor Legions moving forward.

Jackson aimed his huge superhuman gun and smashed down the steel door. Storming out onto the landing platform.

He saw Sarah immediately just standing there in the middle of the immense circular landing platform. The greyness of the platform matched her grey cloak perfectly and she was smiling as she looked up at the sky.

Jackson activated his orbital visual filters and noticed there were thousands upon thousands of

Empire Army warships in high orbit. He had no idea what lie she had told them but it was clear she knew how the Empire worked perfectly.

There had to be a million or more Empire Army soldiers and unless he acted soon they were all going to die.

He really wanted them all to die. He wanted the Empire to suffer a crippling lost, he wanted the loyalists to die and he wanted the so-called traitors to win. But not at the cost of his own life and the lost of the knowledge that Sarah (of all people) had promised him.

Jackson fired.

Bullets screamed towards Sarah.

The bullets slammed into a crystal clear shield around her and Sarah looked at Jackson and Gianna for a moment.

"You two are very obsessed with me. It isn't healthy," Sarah said bringing down the holographic computer system.

"Stop!" Gianna shouted.

"No," Sarah said. "As soon as I activate this computer system the lasers that I have changed will focus on the planet's core,"

"Then you are a monster," Gianna said. "Because the laws of Thermal Expansion will make the liquid expand and break apart the planet's crust,"

"And my personal favourite," Sarah said, "is that when the magma reaches the nuclear weapons you have in the research complex. The entire planet goes bang!"

Jackson fired again.

Bullets shrieked towards Sarah.

The bullets slammed into her shield.

Jackson charged.

He flew at Sarah.

Sarah whipped out a holographic sword. She swung it.

Jackson dodged it.

Tackling her to the ground.

Sarah whacked him across the face. Jackson felt off her.

Sarah leapt up.

Ramming her sword into Jackson's right leg. So far the sword stuck into the landing platform.

Sarah activated the computer systems.

"Lord Commander respond," a man said over Sarah's communication network.

Jackson tried to hack into it and he managed it first time.

"Captain," Jackson said. "This is Ignis Angel Captain Sadie this is a massive deception by the Raven Crow,"

He was going to continue but then he heard the maddening cackle of Sarah's laughter in his ear. He hadn't hacked into the communication network she had only allowed him to think that.

"Help me, help me Captain," Sarah said into her communication device. "The aliens are breaking through and they are devouring the research pores. If they escape the planet alive then they will become a violent tide purging the Empire of all life,"

"Of course we are coming," the man said.

Sarah laughed as she cut the link. "Humans really are a waste of space,"

Jackson grabbed the handle of the holographic blade that was still in his leg and he screamed in agony as it electrocuted him.

He didn't give up.

Through crippling pain Jackson ripped the sword out of his leg and he crushed the handle with his bare hands.

He stood up and Sarah actually wobbled slightly. Superhuman hormones and drugs flooded his body.

"How long do we have to stop the destruction?" Jackson asked.

Gianna shook her head. "Five minutes,"

"For the Lord of War!" Jackson shouted as he charged at Sarah.

He flew at Sarah.

He leapt into the air.

He fired.

Bullets slammed into Sarah.

Throwing her backwards.

Sarah activated her grey cloak.

Jackson couldn't see her. He didn't care. He fired.

Bullets screamed through the air.

Slamming into Sarah.

Knocking her back tens of metres.

Jackson rushed over to her.

Kicking her in the stomach.

They were so close to the edge.

Jackson fired again.

Bullets roared towards Sarah.

They smashed into her stomach.

Knocking her off the platform.

Jackson went over to the edge of the platform to make sure she was falling but he didn't see anything.

A foot kicked him in the back.

He fell forward.

He fell over the edge.

He gripped onto the edge of the platform.

He saw Gianna was standing there smiling at him.

"I am not a fool," she said. "Sarah's dead now and I have to stop you from getting any of the research,"

A bullet shrieked through Gianna.

She screamed as the bullet flew through her chest.

She collapsed to the ground and Jackson saw Sarah standing there.

Sarah came over to him. "Humans seriously never learn or care about what I am capable of. You did manage to break the computer system so thanks for that,"

Jackson was glad they had stopped something.

"But I did remember the nuclear bombs for a reason. Goodbye little superhuman. We will not be seeing each other anymore,"

Jackson's eyes widened as Sarah teleported away and he felt immense vibrations rip through the planet as the nuclear bombs went off.

He had to escape now.

CHAPTER 18

As the bullet smashed in her chest and she saw Sarah teleport off Gianna flat out couldn't believe how stupid, pathetic and dumb she had been. She had always wanted to be the smartest person in the room, always wanted to be the best researcher, always wanted to create something that would save the Empire.

She hadn't wanted to die forgotten on some stupid research planet that was never published in a great journal.

Searing pain burnt through her chest and Gianna watched the droplets of blood pour out of her chest.

She hissed in pain as the immense vibrations of the nuclear bombs ripped through the planet. The nearest bomb was hundreds of miles away but they were around the planet in perfect positions to make it crack.

The planet was going to be wrecked Gianna understood that but there was still a chance for them to live. She might get cancer from the radiation but… then Gianna realised what had really happened about her family for the first time ever.

Sarah Oddballa was not an honourable woman. She wasn't a friend. She wasn't a good person.

Sarah Oddballa had never paid for her family's medical care and Gianna supposed if she wasn't such a workaholic she would have realised there was a simple reason why she hadn't heard from her family for years maybe decades. She actually didn't know anymore.

Her family was dead. Sarah had probably killed them as soon as she had recruited her.

Gianna had to live and find a way to get revenge.

Gianna took deep painful breaths of the intensely cold air as she crawled over to the edge of the platform where Jackson was hanging from.

She offered him a hand. "I'm sorry. We have to survive this and we have to work together,"

Jackson laughed and simply swung himself and his immense superhuman bulk back onto the platform.

He pointed his gun straight at Gianna's head. "You tried to kill me. You tried to end me. I can survive radiation but you cannot. Why should I help you?"

Gianna smiled because he was right. Ever since the superhumans had arrived she had tried to kill them, get rid of them and she thought she was better than them. Maybe she was in some ways but not all.

A deafening roar in the distance screamed overhead as research buildings collapsed from the fires and explosions that were devouring the world.

"I don't have anything to offer the traitors," Gianna said, "but we are both humans. You understand the want to live,"

Jackson lowered the gun and looked around and nodded to himself. "You're going to see exactly how we infiltrate in the Raven Crow Legion,"

Gianna grinned because she had a feeling that this was going to be an immense learning opportunity.

"The communication networks are back up now that Sarah's gone," Jackson said and he looked up towards the battle force.

Gianna really hoped whatever he was planning was actually going to work.

"Captain this is Ignis Angel Jackson. We have been deceived by the Raven Crow. There are no aliens, no nothing. We need immediate extraction from our coordinates,"

"If there are no aliens then why?" a male human asked.

"The Raven Crow have rigged the planet to blow. We have to get us off the planet and I have to protect the Research master,"

"Standby,"

Jackson cut the line as three more research complexes smashed down around them. The ground shook violently.

Gianna fell against Jackson and he lightly gripped her shoulder.

"I'm going to have to report you once onboard," Gianna said.

Jackson nodded and he undid his helmet. Gianna was surprised by the sheer humanity, warmth and kindness of his face. She understood why the Raven Crow were such effective spies, they actually looked friendly compared to other baseline humans and even superhumans.

"I am a Raven Crow and I will survive. By the time your *report* has left your lips I will already be gone," Jackson said.

"So you aren't going to kill me?" Gianna asked.

She held onto Jackson even tighter as the landing platform shook violently and the roar of flames filled the air as did the aromas of burning flesh, rubber and plastic.

"No you are not dying today!" Jackson shouted as he grabbed her and they both jumped off the landing platform.

Gianna screamed as the landing platform exploded and the research complex came smashing down.

Thick columns of black smoke filled her senses and then they stopped and Gianna realised they had both safely been extracted using teleportation and they were now both on a warship in high orbit.

Gianna fell to her knees as the searing pain of her chest wound returned and she just looked at Jackson.

Maybe she could give him a little time to escape. He had saved her life after all, something he seriously didn't have to do.

But as the medical staff took her away to be assessed and healed, she smiled at Jackson and he smiled back. It was never going to be the type of smile a human gave a friend, a bestie or a family member but it was the type of smile that reflected a bond forged in the fires of war and chaos and deceit. And Gianna realised that for the first time in her life, she actually did have a connection with someone that real.

Sure it was with a traitor, someone she could never ever see again but she liked Jackson, and she really hoped he lived a long happy life. Because he was a good man at heart and that meant something to her.

So she was going to give him a little head start, she was going to protect him a little and she was going to go back to researching ways to help rehabilitate traitor superhumans. She knew Jackson would never turn on his foul traitor Masters but the idea excited her a lot more than she ever wanted to admit.

Her family might have been dead but she still had purpose, a life and a lot of amazing things she wanted to explore. And Gianna felt alive for the first time in ages, all because of a crazy woman and a Raven Crow Operative that had infiltrated her life, her heart and her mind.

CHAPTER 19

Sarah Oddballa just watched as Gianna was taken to the medical wing of the ship and she just smiled. Not because she wanted to harm dear Gianna, not because she cared about her but because it was just funny to realise that everything was now over.

She had already activated her grey cloak again as she leant against the icy coldness of a grey metal wall. Tons of men and women in their black Empire Army uniform rushed up and down and through the archway in front of her.

Sarah was half-tempted to grab one of them and see what was happening but she wasn't stupid. The Empire Army was probably wanting to hunt down the Raven Crow threat on the planet and make sure they didn't escape. Sarah was a little surprised that dumb Gianna hadn't revealed who Jackson really was and if Sarah cared even a little bit then maybe she would have confessed and told the Captain of the Battle Force everything.

But there was no fun in that.

Sarah turned around and elegantly glided through the immense sea of Empire Army soldiers, she hated the hints of sweat, oil and grease that poured off them, but they had served their purpose well.

The Battle Force was here and no longer focusing on her. They were chasing ghosts and demons and shadows which meant Sarah could "borrow" a shuttle without anyone noticing. It was perfect really.

Sarah continued going up the corridor and she just grinned at her stash of goodies. She had some blood samples, two Angel fingers and a lot of research for her to devour and learn from.

Sarah wasn't sure what she was going to use them all for but she had a plan (maybe?) and she was one, or maybe five steps, closer to achieving her goal. She was going to win this war for herself and then she was going to free the galaxy of the monsters that raced around in it.

Or was she?

Because that was the thing about Sarah Oddballa. She was a liar, a deceiver and she didn't know fact from fiction most of the time. She wasn't sure if most of the events of the past two days had actually happened, she might have been able to ask Gianna and Jackson what really happened, but there was no fun in that.

And she was crazy and she loved it.

But she was Sarah Oddballa and everything she

ever said was a lie.

CHAPTER 20

About an hour later, Jackson was rather surprised by how easy it had been to steal a fiery red blade-like shuttle from one of the various hangars and zoom off into the void. He had already destroyed the various tracking pieces of software that would allow the evil Empire to follow him and he just looked forward to reuniting with his legion once more.

Jackson sat in the perfectly warm and toasty cockpit on a metal chair with a wide range of holograms, buttons and switches all around him. He had set the shuttle to autopilot and it was speeding through the void to get back with the local Raven Crow legion fleet.

He was so looking forward to finally seeing his friends and legion brothers and sisters again. They could tell each other about their latest missions, share the rewards and most importantly learn from each other.

Jackson watched on all the thousands upon

thousands of stars in the distance that shone like bright beacons towards him. And if he was being reckless then he might have aimed for one and just explored, like how a moth would to a flame, but he had his Legion to focus on.

He wasn't a fan of the bleach, oranges and grapefruit aromas that must have followed him from the research planet, but it was almost comforting in a way. It reminded him of Research Master Gianna, a very complex and weird woman but a person with a good heart.

He hoped she was okay and no one ever learnt the truth about her, but if they did Jackson might watch her and hopefully convert her to the Raven Crow cause once the Empire came after her. And they would because the Empire was evil.

It really was that simple.

Jackson activated the holographic overlays in his helmet and he started reading all the information he had downloaded over the past few hours. As soon as he had started racing up the stairs towards the landing platform he had started to download it all.

It seemed that the death of everyone and the chaos Sarah had caused had made the security systems shut down, so all that wonderful information was available for extraction.

Jackson had to admit there was a lot of cool stuff in the files that would transform the so-called traitor war effort. They could build new weapons, new shields, new everything to crush the Empire with, but there was a single file that interested him.

Sarah hadn't lied.

Jackson opened the file that contained the original research done by Doctor Catherine Taylor and the Emperor himself. It contained everything the Raven Crow Legion needed to start rebuilding itself with new superhumans. This had the power to change everything. Jackson couldn't understand even 1% of it but he knew the signs of good, real and amazing research. This was certainly it.

His hearts pounded in his chest, his stomachs filled with butterflies and Jackson just grinned. There was a hope for a better future and hope for a future where the Lord of War ruled humanity with an iron grip and the Emperor was dead.

Now that was certainly a future Jackson couldn't wait to see and he would finally be the hero he had always wanted to be. Because he would be remembered as the person who rediscovered Angel technology, but there was a single thing that concerned him.

He had checked the files and the dates attached several times but Sarah hadn't changed a single detail. He doubted Sarah was a traitor and he really doubted she was a fan of the Empire, she always had an agenda or a plan.

So why help him find a lost form of technology that could spell the end of the Empire?

It made no sense but as he realised the Raven Crow fleet was scanning him, Jackson just smiled because it didn't matter. He was safe, he was home and he had returned from an infiltration mission with information that would transform the fate of the galaxy forever.

And Jackson was thrilled to have been that deadly force of change.

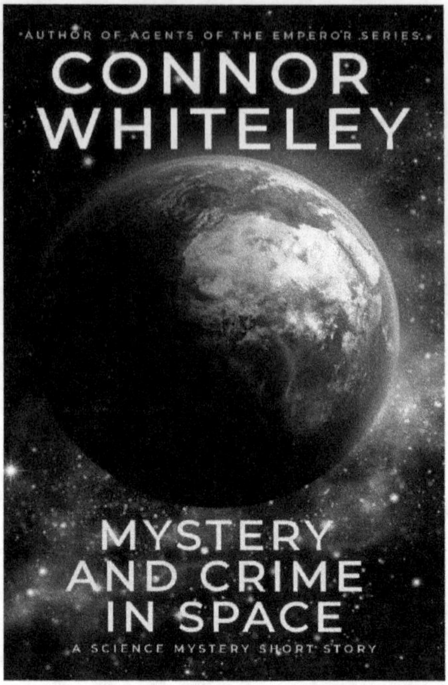

GET YOUR FREE SHORT STORY NOW!
And get signed up to Connor Whiteley's newsletter to hear about new gripping books, offers and exciting projects. (You'll never be sent spam)
https://www.subscribepage.io/garrosignup

About the author:

Connor Whiteley is the author of over 60 books in the sci-fi fantasy, nonfiction psychology and books for writer's genre and he is a Human Branding Speaker and Consultant.

He is a passionate warhammer 40,000 reader, psychology student and author.

Who narrates his own audiobooks and he hosts The Psychology World Podcast.

All whilst studying Psychology at the University of Kent, England.

Also, he was a former Explorer Scout where he gave a speech to the Maltese President in August 2018 and he attended Prince Charles' 70th Birthday Party at Buckingham Palace in May 2018.

Plus, he is a self-confessed coffee lover!

Other books by Connor Whiteley:

Bettie English Private Eye Series

A Very Private Woman
The Russian Case
A Very Urgent Matter
A Case Most Personal
Trains, Scots and Private Eyes
The Federation Protects
Cops, Robbers and Private Eyes
Just Ask Bettie English
An Inheritance To Die For
The Death of Graham Adams
Bearing Witness
The Twelve
The Wrong Body
The Assassination Of Bettie English
Wining And Dying
Eight Hours
Uniformed Cabal
A Case Most Christmas

Gay Romance Novellas

Breaking, Nursing, Repairing A Broken Heart
Jacob And Daniel
Fallen For A Lie
Spying And Weddings
Clean Break

Awakening Love
Meeting A Country Man
Loving Prime Minister
Snowed In Love
Never Been Kissed
Love Betrays You

Lord of War Origin Trilogy:
Not Scared Of The Dark
Madness
Burn Them All

Way Of The Odyssey
Odyssey of Rebirth
Convergence of Odysseys

Lady Tano Fantasy Adventure Stories
Betrayal
Murder
Annihilation

The Fireheart Fantasy Series
Heart of Fire
Heart of Lies
Heart of Prophecy
Heart of Bones
Heart of Fate

City of Assassins (Urban Fantasy)
City of Death
City of Martyrs
City of Pleasure
City of Power

Agents of The Emperor
Return of The Ancient Ones
Vigilance
Angels of Fire
Kingmaker
The Eight
The Lost Generation
Hunt
Emperor's Council
Speaker of Treachery
Birth Of The Empire
Terraforma
Spaceguard

The Rising Augusta Fantasy Adventure Series
Rise To Power
Rising Walls
Rising Force
Rising Realm

Lord Of War Trilogy (Agents of The Emperor)
Not Scared Of The Dark
Madness
Burn It All Down

Miscellaneous:
RETURN
FREEDOM
SALVATION
Reflection of Mount Flame
The Masked One
The Great Deer
English Independence

OTHER SHORT STORIES BY CONNOR WHITELEY

Mystery Short Story Collections
Criminally Good Stories Volume 1: 20 Detective Mystery Short Stories
Criminally Good Stories Volume 2: 20 Private Investigator Short Stories
Criminally Good Stories Volume 3: 20 Crime Fiction Short Stories
Criminally Good Stories Volume 4: 20 Science Fiction and Fantasy Mystery Short Stories

Criminally Good Stories Volume 5: 20 Romantic Suspense Short Stories

Connor Whiteley Starter Collections:
Agents of The Emperor Starter Collection
Bettie English Starter Collection
Matilda Plum Starter Collection
Gay Romance Starter Collection
Way Of The Odyssey Starter Collection
Kendra Detective Fiction Starter Collection

Mystery Short Stories:
Protecting The Woman She Hated
Finding A Royal Friend
Our Woman In Paris
Corrupt Driving
A Prime Assassination
Jubilee Thief
Jubilee, Terror, Celebrations
Negative Jubilation
Ghostly Jubilation
Killing For Womenkind
A Snowy Death
Miracle Of Death
A Spy In Rome
The 12:30 To St Pancreas
A Country In Trouble

A Smokey Way To Go
A Spicy Way To GO
A Marketing Way To Go
A Missing Way To Go
A Showering Way To Go
Poison In The Candy Cane
Kendra Detective Mystery Collection Volume 1
Kendra Detective Mystery Collection Volume 2
Mystery Short Story Collection Volume 1
Mystery Short Story Collection Volume 2
Criminal Performance
Candy Detectives
Key To Birth In The Past

Science Fiction Short Stories:
Their Brave New World
Gummy Bear Detective
The Candy Detective
What Candies Fear
The Blurred Image
Shattered Legions
The First Rememberer
Life of A Rememberer
System of Wonder
Lifesaver

Remarkable Way She Died
The Interrogation of Annabella Stormic
Blade of The Emperor
Arbiter's Truth
Computation of Battle
Old One's Wrath
Puppets and Masters
Ship of Plague
Interrogation
Edge of Failure

Fantasy Short Stories:
City of Snow
City of Light
City of Vengeance
Dragons, Goats and Kingdom
Smog The Pathetic Dragon
Don't Go In The Shed
The Tomato Saver
The Remarkable Way She Died
Dragon Coins
Dragon Tea
Dragon Rider

All books in 'An Introductory Series':

Clinical Psychology and Transgender Clients
Clinical Psychology
Careers In Psychology
Psychology of Suicide
Dementia Psychology
Clinical Psychology Reflections Volume 4
Forensic Psychology of Terrorism And Hostage-Taking
Forensic Psychology of False Allegations
Year In Psychology
CBT For Anxiety
CBT For Depression
Applied Psychology
BIOLOGICAL PSYCHOLOGY 3RD EDITION
COGNITIVE PSYCHOLOGY THIRD EDITION
SOCIAL PSYCHOLOGY- 3RD EDITION
ABNORMAL PSYCHOLOGY 3RD EDITION
PSYCHOLOGY OF RELATIONSHIPS- 3RD EDITION
DEVELOPMENTAL PSYCHOLOGY 3RD EDITION
HEALTH PSYCHOLOGY
RESEARCH IN PSYCHOLOGY

A GUIDE TO MENTAL HEALTH AND TREATMENT AROUND THE WORLD- A GLOBAL LOOK AT DEPRESSION

FORENSIC PSYCHOLOGY

THE FORENSIC PSYCHOLOGY OF THEFT, BURGLARY AND OTHER CRIMES AGAINST PROPERTY

CRIMINAL PROFILING: A FORENSIC PSYCHOLOGY GUIDE TO FBI PROFILING AND GEOGRAPHICAL AND STATISTICAL PROFILING.

CLINICAL PSYCHOLOGY

FORMULATION IN PSYCHOTHERAPY

PERSONALITY PSYCHOLOGY AND INDIVIDUAL DIFFERENCES

CLINICAL PSYCHOLOGY REFLECTIONS VOLUME 1

CLINICAL PSYCHOLOGY REFLECTIONS VOLUME 2

Clinical Psychology Reflections Volume 3

CULT PSYCHOLOGY

Police Psychology

www.ingramcontent.com/pod-product-compliance
Lightning Source LLC
La Vergne TN
LVHW012121070526
838202LV00056B/5814